FIZZ WIZZ PHONICS is a series of fun and exciting books, especially designed to be used by children who have not yet started to read.

The books support the development of language, exploring key speaking and listening skills, as well as encouraging confidence in pre-reading skills.

CLAP YOUR HANDS is all about body percussion and the sounds that can be made using different parts of your body. This book includes a selection of well-known action songs. Children will have fun learning the songs, practising the actions to each song and making the noises that accompany the actions shown in the photographs.

For suggestions on how to use **CLAP YOUR HANDS** and for further activities, look at page 24 of this book.

Wind The Bobbin Up

Wind the bobbin up.
Wind the bobbin up.

CLAP YOUR HANDS

Written by

KATE RUTTLE

Illustrated by

MIRIAM LATIMER

WAYLAND

First published in 2011
by Wayland

This paperback edition published
in 2012 by Wayland

Wayland
338 Euston Road
London NW1 3BH

Wayland Australia
Level 17/207 Kent Street
Sydney, NSW 2000

Series editor: Louise John
Designer: Paul Cherrill
Consultant: Kate Ruttle

A CIP catalogue record for this book is available
from the British Library.

ISBN 9780750266505

Printed in China

Wayland is a division of Hachette Children's Books,
an Hachette UK company. www.hachette.co.uk

Wind the bobbin up

Pull, pull!
Clap, clap, clap!

Ten Fat Sausages

Ten fat sausages
sizzling in a pan,

One went POP!
And another went BANG!

Roly Poly

Ro... ly... po... ly... ever... so... slowly.
Ro... ly... poly faster.
Roly poly as fast as you can,
if you want to be master!

Stamp!

Stamp... your... feet... ever... so... slowly.
Stamp... your feet faster.
Stamp your feet as fast as you can,
if you want to be master!

(Increase the speed of the action as you increase the speed of the rhyme.)

In The Garden

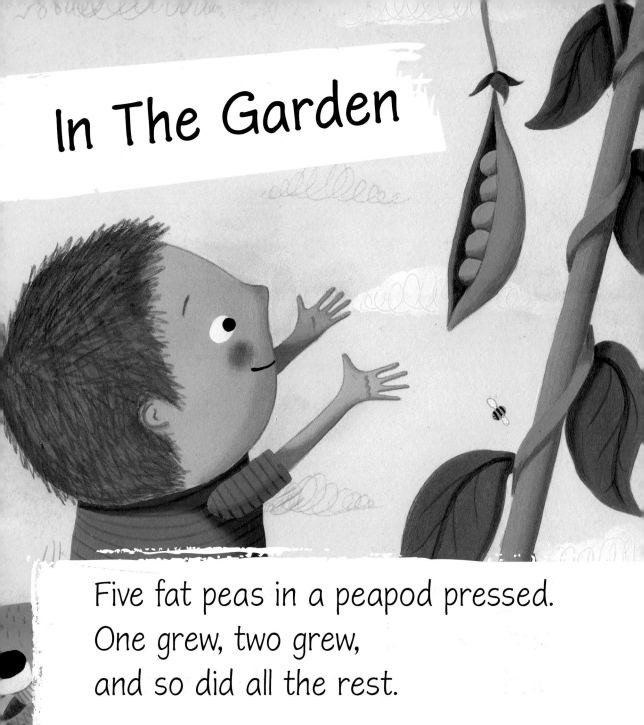

Five fat peas in a peapod pressed.
One grew, two grew,
and so did all the rest.

They grew and they grew,
and they did not stop.
Until, one day, the pod went POP!

Ten Little Fingers

I have ten little fingers,
and they all belong to me.
I can make them do things.
Would you like to see?

Snap, snap!

I can snap them high,
I can flick them low.
I can fold them up quietly,
and hold them just like... so.

13

Horsey, Horsey!

Clip clop, clip clop,
clip clop, clip clop.
Horsey, horsey, don't you stop.
Just let your feet go clippetty-clop.

Your tail goes swish,
and your wheels go round.
Giddy up, we're homeward bound.

Noisy Neighbour!

Up in the bedroom,
early in the morning,
see the sleeping children,
snore snore snoring.

Zzzzz

Suddenly they wake up,
looking all around,
asking all together,
"What's that sound?"

I've Got A Busy Body

I've got a body, a very busy body,
and it goes everywhere with me.
And on that body, I've got two hands,
and they go everywhere with me.

Clap, clap!

With a clap, clap here and a clap, clap there,
a clap, clap, clap everywhere.
I've got a body, a very busy body,
and it goes everywhere with me.

19

Clap Your Hands

Clap your hands together,
together, together.
Clap your hands together,
clap, clap, clap!

Snap your fingers together,
together, together.
Snap your fingers together,
snap, snap, snap!

If You're Happy

If you're happy and you know it,
clap your hands.
If you're happy and you know it,
clap your hands.

If you're happy and you know it,
and you really want to show it.
If you're happy and you know it,
clap your hands.

Further Activities

 These activities can be used
when reading the book one-to-one,
or in the home.

 These activities can be used when
using the book with more than one
child, or in an educational setting.

P4 • Do the actions to this song as you sing along. What sounds do you make with your body as you do the actions?
• Try moving someone else's arms to do the actions as you both sing. Is it easier or harder than using your own body?

P6 • Listen to the sounds you make as you are cooking. Can you mimic the sounds using your voice?

P8 • See how slowly, then how fast, you can speak the words in each verse.

P10 • Hold a fist to make the peapod. Slowly grow one finger, then two fingers at the relevant lines of the song. Separate your hand as the pod is growing fatter, then pop your cheek in the last line.

P12 • Sing the song and do the actions to the rhyme. What sorts of noises do you make with your body as you do the actions?

P14 • Do the actions as you sing the song. Which parts of your body do you use?

P16 • Act out the rhyme with a friend or parent. You can be in one room and your friend can be in another (or behind a chair). One of you should make a sound, such as a snore or a clap and the other can guess what you might be doing.

P18 • Find the song and accompanying music on the Internet. Sing along to the track, doing the actions as you sing.

P20 • Find other verses to this song on the Internet. Using a mirror, do the actions to the song. Look and listen carefully to the noises each action makes.

P22 • Talk about other noises you can make with your body. Can you think of any actions to these noises, too?

P4 • Add the second verse to this song and sing the whole song at the end of the day.

P6 • All line up in a line to be 'sausages'. Can you work out what sound you should make — a 'Pop' or a 'Bang'?

P8 • Try adding new verses, using different parts of the body: clap your hands; nod your head, snap your fingers, knock your knees.

P10 • Look for images of peapods growing and popping on the Internet. Can you mimic the movement and sounds they make?

P12 • Explore what else you can do with your fingers to make a noise, for example try wiggling them when they are rubbing together and when they are separated. What else can you do?

P14 • Look at images of horses on the Internet. Can you hear the 'clip clop' sound they make as they walk? What other noises do horses make?

P16 • Add the other verses to the rhyme and use it to explore miming. Chant the rhyme as you stand up and mime the actions you can hear.

P18 • As you sing the song in a group, try not to sing the words but make the noises. For example instead of saying the word 'clap', do a clap with your hands instead.

P20 • Make a book of the song. Take photographs of your friends doing the actions and stick them in a book. Write each verse underneath a photograph.

P22 • As a group, sing the song together as you move around the room. Add more verses to the song and think about how you would mimic the action and the sound?